W9-BWC-184

12/2018

PALM BEACH COUNTY
LIBRARY SYSTEM
3650 Summit Boulevard
West Palm Beach, FL 33406-4198

Dear Parents:

Congratulations! Your child is taking the first steps on an exciting journey. The destination? Independent reading!

STEP INTO READING® will help your child get there. The program offers five steps to reading success. Each step includes fun stories and colorful art or photographs. In addition to original fiction and books with favorite characters, there are Step into Reading Non-Fiction Readers, Phonics Readers and Boxed Sets, Sticker Readers, and Comic Readers—a complete literacy program with something to interest every child.

Learning to Read, Step by Step!

Ready to Read   Preschool–Kindergarten
• big type and easy words • rhyme and rhythm • picture clues
For children who know the alphabet and are eager to begin reading.

Reading with Help   Preschool–Grade 1
• basic vocabulary • short sentences • simple stories
For children who recognize familiar words and sound out new words with help.

Reading on Your Own   Grades 1–3
• engaging characters • easy-to-follow plots • popular topics
For children who are ready to read on their own.

Reading Paragraphs   Grades 2–3
• challenging vocabulary • short paragraphs • exciting stories
For newly independent readers who read simple sentences with confidence.

Ready for Chapters   Grades 2–4
• chapters • longer paragraphs • full-color art
For children who want to take the plunge into chapter books but still like colorful pictures.

STEP INTO READING® is designed to give every child a successful reading experience. The grade levels are only guides; children will progress through the steps at their own speed, developing confidence in their reading. The F&P Text Level on the back cover serves as another tool to help you choose the right book for your child.

Remember, a lifetime love of reading starts with a single step!

To Joanna B. Hills—a gift to many

Duck & Goose
A Gift for Goose

Tad Hills

Random House 🏠 New York

Duck has a gift
for Goose.

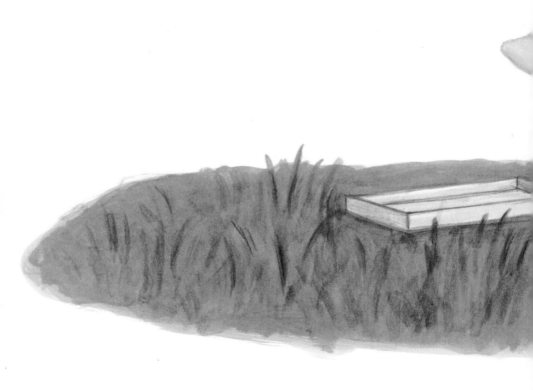

He puts it in a box.

He closes the box.

He paints it red,
yellow, and blue.

He waits
for the paint
to dry.

Duck makes a card.

He puts a blue ribbon
on the box.

"What is that?"

Goose honks.

"It is a gift for you,"
Duck quacks.

"For me?

Thank you!

It is the nicest box

I have ever seen!"

honks Goose.

"But . . . ," Duck quacks.

"I can put my special
things in the box,"
Goose honks.

"But . . . ," Duck quacks.

"I will go and get
my special things,"
honks Goose.

"But . . . wait,"
Duck quacks.

Goose gets his crayons,

his shell,

and his winter hat
and scarf.

He gets his summer hat

and his ball of yarn

to put in the box.

"But, Goose,"
Duck says.
"This box is not
your gift."

"What?" honks Goose.

"It is not mine?"

"No. Your gift is <u>inside</u>
this box,"
Duck quacks.

Goose opens the box.

He looks inside.

Goose pulls out a
polka-dotted box.
"It is a box! I love it!"
he honks.

"It is for your special
things," quacks Duck.

"Thank you, Duck. It is
the nicest box I have
ever seen!" honks Goose.